Daytona!

THUNDER AT THE BEACH

BY JAY SCHLEIFER

CRESTWOOD HOUSE
PARSIPPANY, NEW JERSEY
Printed in U.S.A.

Acknowledgment

Thanks to Al Seyfer and the Tampa region of Safety-Kleen Corporation for their help in arranging a visit to Daytona and in researching this book.

Copyright © 1995 by Silver Burdett Press

All rights reserved. No part of this book may be reproduced or transmitted in any form or by any means, electronic or mechanical, including photocopying, recording, or by any information storage and retrieval system, without written permission in writing from the Publisher.

Published by Crestwood House, an imprint of Silver Burdett Press.
A Simon & Schuster Company
299 Jefferson Road, Parsippany, N.J. 07054

First Edition

Produced by Twelfth House Produtions
Designed by R studio T

Photo Credits:
cover: Daytona International Speedway
International Speedway Corporation: 5, 13, 24, 29, 42
Daytona Racing Archives: 9, 11, 19, 26, 32-33, 38-39
Daytona International Speedway: 17, 21, 45

Printed in the United States of America
10 9 8 7 6 5 4 3 2 1

LIBRARY OF CONGRESS CATALOGING-IN-PUBLICATION DATA

Schleifer, Jay.
   Daytona : thunder at the beach / by Jay Schleifer.
     p.   cm.— (Out to win)
   Includes index.
   ISBN 0-89686-818-4
   1. Daytona International Speedway Race—Juvenile Literature.
I. Title. II. Series.
GV1033.5.D39S35 1995   94-28496
796.7'2'0975921—dc20

CONTENTS

1	Riding the Thunder Train	4
2	Speed and Sand	6
3	Home of the Land Speed Record	8
4	Bootlegger Beach	10
5	Taking the Heat	16
6	"Pops"	18
7	Superspeedway!	20
8	Formula for Success	23
9	King Richard the Fast!	25
10	Car Wars	28
11	A Matter of Engine-ering	34
12	The "Tide" of Victory	36
13	Pit Action	41
14	Future Stock!	43
15	Race Day!	44

Glossary   46
Index   48

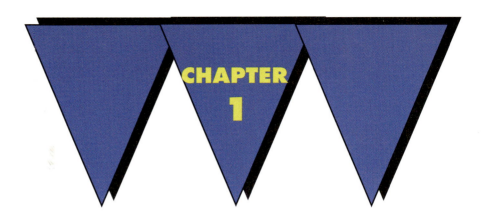

CHAPTER 1

RIDING THE THUNDER TRAIN

The race cars barrel out of pit lane all in a row. They blast onto the track, nose to tail. A second later they form a nine-car streak. As they pick up speed, their monster 700-horsepower V-8 engines tear at the air. They sound like rolling thunder.

You're at the wheel of the fourth car in this high-speed express train. Your racer carries the same name as your mom's street sedan: Chevy Lumina. But take our word for it, this is not your mother's Lumina.

The steering wheel in your hands is removable. You're belted to a special formfitting seat. And you're looking through a **Lexan** *plastic windshield that's tough enough to stop a bullet. It's also strengthened with metal rods so it won't cave in when you're driving 200 mph. This is hardly a family car.*

As you roar down the track, the **banking** *of turn 1 looms in front of you like the wall of a cliff. How can any car cross that rock face without sliding off?*

You don't have much time to wonder. Almost as quickly as you see it, you're on it.

Suddenly your world goes sideways as your racer slants to follow the slope of the road. The banked track works as it's supposed to. You're doing better than 150 mph, but turning forces glue you and your car to the wall like a squashed bug. You hardly have to slow down. The track flattens again and you're into the back straight—the fastest part

Daytona's "thunder trains" began when drivers discovered that a line of cars cuts through the air more easily than one racer alone.

of the track.

    Car 3 in the chain is right in front of you. You close in on its bumper. Suddenly you feel as though a giant hand is pulling you forward. It's the **draft** from the three vehicles ahead. This wind effect drags you along *like a dustball into a vacuum cleaner.*

The speed of the whole chain gets faster than any car would go alone. You hit 170. Then 180. Then 190. And, finally, 200. And you haven't given the car much gas. The chain of cars just seems to have a mind of its own.

The straight flashes by. Then the banking puts you sideways again, faster than before. This is probably what an F-15 pilot feels during a dogfight. But in a dogfight, the other planes are more than 18 inches away.

As the road flattens back into the pit straight, you head into pit lane. You ease the four jumbo disk brakes to a smooth stop. And then you smile.

*You've just run one practice lap at the Daytona International Speedway. You drove a **Winston Cup** stock car, a **NASCAR** machine! Tomorrow you're going to run 200 of these 2 1/2-mile-long trips around the track. You're an experienced, careful driver. But are you ready for the heat and pressure of the Daytona 500?*

CHAPTER 2

SPEED AND SAND

Every year more than 150,000 fans attend the Daytona 500 in sunny Florida. But racing at Daytona Beach didn't actually start at Daytona Beach. It began in Ormand Beach, 12 miles up the Florida coast.

In the early 1900s, Ormand was a winter playground for the rich and famous. Inclued in that group were Alexander Winton and Ransom E. Olds—two of America's first auto factory owners. Winton built a car of the same name. Olds invented—you guessed it—the *Olds*mobile, now made by General Motors. He also created the Reo truck.

One winter, Olds was looking for a fun way to pass the time. He came up with the idea of running one of his cars right on the beach. The area between Ormand and Daytona has a strip of flat, hard sand that's kept smooth by the tide. It's more than 20 miles long. Most U.S. roads at the time were mud tracks. In comparison, the beach at Daytona must have seemed like a superhighway.

Olds was eager to know how fast his car could go. So he had the run timed as he putt-putted down the shining shoreline. Soon afterward, he cornered his friend Winton. "Alex," he said breathlessly, "you have no idea what a thrill it is to go 50 miles an hour!"

Soon Winton had tried the thrill himself. Then he and Olds decided to hold a race. They ran side by side all the way from Ormand to Daytona and back. They hit an incredible (for the time) 57 mph. And since both men were gentlemen, they agreed to cross the finish line in a tie.

When reports of the race spread, people sensed a new way to attract visitors. Town officials decided to hold a yearly "speed week." But the races that followed were a lot faster—and a lot less gentlemanly—than the officials had ever imagined.

HOME OF THE LAND SPEED RECORD

In the years that followed, Daytona became the place where people tried to break the world's Land Speed Record. From roughly 1910 through 1936, daredevil drivers raced the world's most powerful cars on Daytona Beach. Each had the goal of becoming the fastest human on wheels.

One of the most famous to try for this record was a young American, Frank Lockhart. There were also two British kings of speed, Major Henry O. Seagrave and Sir Malcolm Campbell.

Lockhart's story is a sad one. Driving a Stutz Blackhawk special, he had all the courage of his rich British rivals. But he didn't have their bank accounts. To cut costs, he disobeyed a key rule of speed runs. He didn't change the tires after each try.

On a 1928 run, at more than 200 mph, a tire that had been run too fast and too often blew out. It launched Lockhart's car on a 1,000-foot end-over-end roll.

Officials raced to the scene but arrived too late to do anything. Lockhart had saved the cost of a tire at the cost of his life.

Seagrave and Campbell picked up where Lockhart left off. They drove high-powered cars named Golden Arrow and Bluebird. Each in turn raised

Britain's Sir Malcolm Campbell in the aircraft-engined Bluebird. Note the open cockpit and leather helmet.

the world mark to new heights. In 1930, the record had reached 231 mph. Then the news came that Seagrave had died in a speedboat crash. (He was trying to be the first human to hold both the land and water speed records at the same time.) Campbell decided to carry on alone.

But Sir Malcolm wanted to do more than just raise the record to 240 or 250. He announced that he would be the first human to drive a car at 300 mph! And he'd do it in a new version of the Bluebird on the sands of Daytona.

Campbell's new car appeared at the beach in 1935. It boasted a gigantic 22-liter engine. Designed to power a plane, the engine pumped more than 2,500 horsepower. The car's body was roughly 27 feet long. It was fitted with advanced air flaps and fins. The gearbox had only three speeds and didn't shift out of low gear until 170 mph—and it didn't shift into high gear until 240 mph!

In trying for the new record, Campbell roared across the sands over and over again. But sand that seems smooth at 50 or 60 mph is amazingly rough at over 200. The Bluebird spent almost as much time flying off bumps as it did gaining speed on the ground.

Finally, on March 5, 1935, Campbell accepted 276.82 mph as the best he could do at Daytona. Then he went off to find a smoother, less crowded place to race. That place turned out to be the great salt flats at Bonneville, Utah. Six months later, he hit 301.13 mph.

When Campbell left Daytona, a quiet settled over the town. The city's days as a speed record capital were over. And citizens worried that their famous sands might turn into just another Florida beach.

They need not have worried. A great new era was about to begin.

CHAPTER 4

BOOTLEGGER BEACH

The street that runs up to the entrance of the Daytona International Speedway is called Bill France Boulevard. There's a good reason for it: Bill France was the first president of the National Association for Stock Car Auto Racing. It's the group that sponsors the yearly Daytona

500 and dozens of other stock car races. But France was more than just a NASCAR official. He had founded NASCAR. In many minds, he *was* NASCAR.

Back in 1934, Bill France was just a dirt-poor car mechanic and part-time racer. Born in Washington, D.C., he'd spent many Saturday nights there, driving jalopy racers around local tracks. But when they had a child, France and his wife decided it was time for a new start. So they packed up their things and moved to sunny Florida.

"I had $25 in my pocket, $75 in the bank, and a set of old tools," Bill said later. "A lot of stories said my car broke down and that's why we set-

Daytona's first stock car races were run right on the beach.

tled in Daytona. But that's not true. I could have fixed it. I just liked Daytona."

What France liked about Daytona was the beach. France had heard of the great speed runs of Lockhart, Seagrave, and Campbell. So when he realized he was passing through Daytona, he just had to drive down the same sand they had. After one ride, he was hooked.

As a Daytona citizen, Bill helped talk city officials into building a 3.2-mile oval track. The track would be half on the sand and half on the beach road next to it. The city also agreed to put up prize money for a 250-mile race.

But what kind of cars should race at Daytona?

One choice was open-wheel machines like those that ran at Indy. Open-wheel cars are built for high-speed racing and have four wheels that are completely exposed to the air. Another idea was to run expensive European sports cars, like Bugatti or Alfa Romeo.

At the time, America was in the middle of the Depression. Nobody had much money, so the decision was easy to make. France's group decided to let people race the same cars they used for everyday transportation—mostly Fords and Chevies.

France knew that regular cars (or "street cars," as they're called) would also attract fans. Average Americans could root for a Ford or a Chevy in a way that they could never root for a Bugatti. The new race would be limited to stock cars.

But some officials worried that such a race wouldn't be exciting enough. Were there enough fast stock cars and skilled stock car drivers to put on a great show? And where would these budding young race organizers find them?

The answer turned out to be closer than anyone had imagined. Stock car racing had already gotten a strong start in several neighboring southern states. In fact, it had grown out of an illegal business called **bootlegging.**

During the 1920s the selling of liquor was outlawed. So secret backwoods factories started selling alcohol to people in the cities. This was a big moneymaking business. But getting the stuff to the city wasn't easy. Police and government officials were waiting to arrest anybody who transported alcohol.

Daredevil drivers called bootleggers were the transporters. (These people got their name from the fact that they sometimes hid illegal liquor inside a set of high boots.)

Whatever can be said about the bootleggers, they certainly could drive! They packed their cars full of illegal liquors. Then they sped down narrow

Chevies and Fords are still hot, but they no longer run on the beach...and the cars are no longer street models!

country roads at night—sometimes driving without lights!

Hauling a load of liquor was no small task. Just 150 gallons added 1,000 pounds to a car's weight. It dragged down the speed on hills and upset the handling. The bootleggers had to learn how to hot-rod a car to get performance back. But the vehicle had to look like a regular car. The bootleggers didn't want to attract attention.

On days off, bootleggers honed their driving skills by racing each other through fields and mudflats. Then some graduated to local tracks in Georgia and other states.

Bill France put out the word that he needed stock car drivers. And it didn't take long for the bootleggers of Georgia and the Carolinas to hear his call. For them, it was a hop, a skip, and a jump to Daytona's sandy speedway. Some even said the best racing was not at Daytona but on the way to Daytona.

The first race on the new Daytona Beach racetrack was held in 1936. It was a shaky start. Not all local leaders supported it, and a few actually tried to ruin the event! One hid the prize money for a while. Another swiped the tickets. The race was run, but thousands of fans got in free.

The race itself was just as much a mess as the preparation. Cars got bogged down in the sand. The turns became a rutted nightmare. And the scorers lost track of who was leading. Finally a winner was named, but Bill France later said, "How they figured out who won, I don't know."

By 1938, most of the people who'd set up the first race had moved on. France was left to continue the races. And he knew he needed help.

At first, France tried to phone an outside expert. But because France didn't have any change on hand, he decided to call the man collect. But the expert refused to pay for the call from his end.

So France looked for help from a few local people. Together, they organized the race. Later, France claimed it was that lack of coins that put him into the race-organizing business full-time.

France had a talent for the work. He figured out ways to smooth the sand, fill in the ruts, and score the races. He also started inspections to solve a major problem in stock car racing: car builders who cheated.

Over the years, the builders showed what truly creative cheaters they were. One hollowed out his car's frame and loaded the empty spots with BB's. When the inspectors weighed the car, the weight was legal. But as soon as the race began, the driver pulled a secret lever. The BB's poured out, making the car lighter.

Another builder mounted the rear bumper with thin wire. He knew that cars often bumped into one another during the race. At the first nudge from a following car, the bumper magically broke off, leaving the racer lighter and more streamlined.

Perhaps the granddaddy of all cheats was the "gasoline basketball." The crew chief sneaked a ball into a fuel tank that held more gas than was allowed. When the ball was full of air, the tank held the legal amount of fuel. But once inspectors were gone, the air was let out of the ball. Suddenly the tank could hold more gas. And that meant the car could skip pit stops. The trick was discovered when somebody calculated the car's gas mileage. It was getting 132 miles of racing from a single tank of gas!

Rules seemed made to be broken on the track as well. "Those early races were heartstoppers," remembers one longtime fan. "When the flag dropped, the drivers went through the pits, in the grass, in the infield, anywhere! If you didn't get out of the way, they'd run right over you!"

But in spite of all the problems, racing at Daytona improved over the next few years. Then, when the United States entered World War II in 1941, the lights went out at tracks across the country. For a time, the only speed that mattered was the speed used to dodge bullets and charge the enemy. Then, in 1945, the war ended. It was time to start racing again.

CHAPTER 5

TAKING THE HEAT

As you prepare for the big race tomorrow, you think about the other drivers. Many are newcomers. And not all drivers are men. Several women have tried the big stockers out. Janet Guthrie raced at Daytona in 1977, finishing twelfth.

Family teams and father-and-son racing are both NASCAR traditions. But these days brother acts are a feature. Geoff and Brett Bodine, Terry and Bobby LaBonte, and Kenny and Rusty Wallace give new meaning to the term "family feud" when they're out on the track.

Today's drivers are cool, classy, and professional. They have to be. Stock car racing is dangerous, and drivers have to use both wisdom and common sense when they're behind the wheel.

Many of today's drivers are world famous. But most are still down-to-earth and easy to talk to. They welcome you as a rookie. They tell you some great stories. And they give you some racing tips. But even they can't prepare you for what's ahead. Driving a stocker is not easy. The typical race involves two or three hours of intense heat and pressure. Cabin heat can rise to over 120 degrees Fahrenheit on a hot summer day. Some drivers almost faint from the heat. And a driver may lose 5 to 10 pounds in a single race! Looking around at the other drivers, you wonder if you've got what it takes.

In 24 hours, you'll know the answer.

The big Florida track was carefully designed to handle high-speed racers.

CHAPTER 6

"POPS"

Stock car racing picked up again after World War II. And there were new faces in many of the drivers' seats. They were typical hometown boys, and some were war heroes.

That was just what the fans wanted. The United States had just spent almost four years fighting in a brutal war. Now it was time for a little fun! And sometimes that fun got pretty wild.

One of the wildest drivers was Curtis "Pops" Turner. He earned his nickname for his habit of "popping" (banging into) other race cars if they didn't get out of the way fast enough. Born in Floyd, Virginia, Turner got his start hauling liquor, just like the other bootleggers—except that he was only nine at the time!

As a stock car racer, Turner was amazing. His skill showed most clearly on the dirt or sand tracks of the time. Fans still talk about how he roared through the turns at high speeds. "The laws of nature just didn't seem to apply to him," wrote one fan. "I'd pay to see him even if he never won!" said another.

But he won—and won—and won. In 1956 Turner took 22 of the 43 races he entered. He followed up by winning 11 of 31 the next year. Top teams fought to have him as a driver, even though he was hard to manage.

Curtis "Pops" Turner was one of NASCAR'S first and wildest superstars.

    The Holly Farms racing team learned firsthand that Pops had a mind of his own. The team had decided to have all its members wear uniforms. Pops was told to wear the driver's suit the team gave him instead of his usual sports clothes. Pops obeyed—sort of. He showed up at the race in a three-piece business suit, complete with alligator shoes and a cowboy hat! "They told me Ah had to wear a suit, so Ah wore mah best," Turner told reporters in his deep Southern accent. "Ya gotta look good, ya know."

    Hard-driving, high-living drivers like Curtis Turner were typical of stock car racing of the late 1940s and 50s. But they were the last of their breed. Big changes were about to happen in Daytona, and to the rest of the stock car world. The good ol' boys were about to make the major leagues.

CHAPTER 7

SUPERSPEEDWAY!

As the 1950s ended and the 1960s approached, a big change was taking place in the American car market.
When the soldiers came back from World War II, they'd married and had children. Now those millions of babies were at the age where they could afford cars. Suddenly young people were the most important car buyers in the market. And young car buyers wanted fast, exciting vehicles.

In Detroit the heads of the big car companies noticed the trend. Many realized that stock car racing could make their street machines more exciting. So the companies were prepared to spend millions to help build top cars and back top teams.

First, though, they had to be sure that the racing they backed was clean and well run. The top companies in America didn't want to deal with a bunch of ex-bootleggers!

As it turned out, Bill France was the answer to the automakers' prayers. In 1948 he'd formed the National Association for Stock Car Auto Racing—NASCAR. In time, France's group got the rights to run most of America's top stock car races.

What's more, France was about to do something to show just how big and powerful NASCAR had become. He was about to build the world's first **superspeedway.**

France had known for years that cars could not continue racing on Daytona's sandy beach. The crowds were getting too big. The cars were getting too fast. Million-dollar events couldn't be held up because of changing ocean tides. NASCAR had to have a proper home if it was to grow.

France went to city officials with his plea. Together they agreed to build a monster track like no other. The new track would sit on 455 acres of land. It would be 2 1/2 miles around and hold more than 100,000 people.

The shape would be neither a circle nor an oval. It would be a **trioval**, a kind of rounded triangle shape. The turns would be steeply sloped, or banked, to allow for greater speed. "I wanted our stock cars to be as fast as Indy cars, and with the high banking it was possible," France explained. Anyone who's ever seen a Daytona 500 race knows that France's wish

When the Daytona Speedway was built, there were no others like it in the world!

proved to be more than possible. Cars routinely circle the track at 200 mph!

Work began on the new track in 1957. And it wasn't long before France announced the first major race. The new Daytona International Speedway would open on Washington's Birthday, 1959. The first event was a 500-mile race for late-model stock cars—the first Daytona 500.

As the great day neared, NASCAR officials felt they'd made the right move in building the speedway. But there was still one worry—Florida's wet climate. A rainy day would spoil the opening day, and rain was predicted.

But the forecast was wrong. Instead, 59 cars ran one of the greatest races in history. Most of the cars were sleek, well-prepared Oldsmobiles, Fords, Chevies, and Pontiacs. They were evenly matched and very, very fast. The old beach record was broken in the first trial runs.

Once the race began, the lead kept changing. Three drivers were locked in battle for the first 22 laps. They passed each other again and again. Then the 1950s superstar Glenn "Fireball" Roberts took over for the next 20 laps. At 375 miles, another longtime star, Lee Petty, grabbed the top spot in an Olds 88. But he lost it just five laps later to Ford driver Johnny Beauchamp.

Now Petty and Beauchamp battled it out lap by lap. They often ran fender to fender, as the crowd screamed in delight.

On the last lap, the two were neck and neck in a dash to the finish line. A third car, a lap down, ran right beside them, and all three crossed at what seemed the same instant! The crowds and judges alike were stunned. After 500 miles of incredible racing, nobody was sure who'd won.

The judges couldn't agree on what to do. First they gave the race to Beauchamp. Then they changed their minds and decided the winner was Petty. But just to be sure, they asked to see news photos taken of the finish.

The photos, however, were already on their way to New York to be published. It took three long days to get them back. Finally the judges gave their decision: Lee Petty had won the first Daytona 500 by a matter of inches. It was a finish millions of fans would never forget.

That first race also marked the start of a new era of racing—the superspeedway era. And this new era needed a new kind of driver—a driver who had a more professional approach than the good ol' boys of the dirt and sand track days. Finishing in fifty-seventh place in that first Daytona 500 was such a driver. A 22-year-old rookie at the time, he would later be crowned as king of NASCAR *and* of Daytona. It was Lee Petty's son Richard.

FORMULA FOR SUCCESS

As you lie in bed the night before the race, you remember the day you visited one of the specialist shops. There you saw stock cars being built.

When you arrived, you were amazed. The grease and grime of a regular garage were nowhere to be found.

The car you saw had a built-up **chassis**, *complete with heavy-duty parts. It featured 9-slot, 15-inch wheels and big 12-inch disk brakes on all four wheels. Suspension was a simple coil spring. And the engine poured its power through a Borg-Warner 4-speed gearbox into a fat, 9-inch rear end.*

You were a little surprised that the chassis wasn't fancier. But you knew that the little things could be just as important as the big ones. The specialists **locknutted** *every key nut and bolt. A car has to hold together, no matter how difficult the conditions are on the track.*

The tubular roll cage increases overall strength and protects the driver in a rollover.

With the chassis done, builders welded in the **roll cage**—a framework of heavy metal tubes that would go around and over you when you drove the car. Built correctly, a roll cage can withstand a rollover at 200 mph.

You've seen the horrible crashes that sometimes happen in NASCAR races. And thinking about tomorrow's big race, you're thankful for the roll cage.

You're also thankful for the **fuel cells**. Fuel cells are rubberized bags filled with a special foam that prevents the spread of fire. You know that top drivers have survived crashes only to die in the fires that followed.

As you doze off, you hope that you won't need the roll cage or the fuel cells tomorrow. But you're glad you'll have them, just in case!

KING RICHARD THE FAST!

Look at a map of North Carolina, and you'll have a hard time finding Level Cross. Like many tiny towns, it's too small for map makers to notice. But stock car racing fans know Level Cross. It's the home of King Richard the Fast! Richard Petty.

Petty, who raced for more than 30 years, was NASCAR's winningest driver. He won more Daytona 500s than anyone else. And he piled up an equally strong record wherever stock cars raced. Richard Petty broke free from the old bootlegger style. He was a pro, pure and simple.

Of course, he got a great start by simply being the son of top driver and car builder Lee Petty. But Lee didn't make things easy for his son.

The two raced each other for four years. During that time, Lee's racer days wound down, and Richard's climb to success began. In one race, Richard figured he had an easy win over his dad. But Lee felt there'd been a mistake in the way the laps were counted. He went to the judges and filed a complaint against his own son, taking Richard's victory away.

Richard had no problem with that. "Dad taught me you have to earn everything you get," he said. "They were hard lessons, but I don't regret them."

Richard raced for the first time at Daytona in 1959. By 1964, he had his first win at NASCAR's biggest race. There have been a few two-time Daytona winners, and even a three-timer, Cale Yarborough. But Richard Petty won at Daytona seven times. He might have won an eighth Daytona 500 in 1965. But his sponsor, Chrysler, pulled out of NASCAR over a rules question.

Petty's best years were in the late 1960s. In 1967 he won 27 of NASCAR's top races. No other driver had ever won more than 18 in a year. Included in the total was an incredible run of 10 straight victories. In 1968 he took 16 more trophies. He even achieved two back-to-back wins in a single 18-hour period!

"King" Richard Petty won Daytona seven times and brought a more scientific style of driving. Note the radio for talking to the pit crew.

Petty's driving style was as important as his record. Other drivers slammed and jammed to get and hold the lead. But Richard learned to play it cool, saving his car and himself. He'd wait for the others to make a mistake, and then he'd strike. He got so good at this that some people called him Rattlesnake.

The 1979 Daytona race was a perfect example. Two hotheads were in a wild fight for the lead, with Petty lying back in third. As the race wore on, the duel out front got crazier and crazier. There was a lot of fender bumping and chance taking.

Richard could see that the two leaders were as interested in taking each other out as in winning the race. Finally, on the last turn, both drivers dove for the finish. Neither would give way, even if it meant a crash. Crash they did, with both cars spinning out of control.

Even then the two drivers' private war wasn't over. They left their wrecked cars and started a fistfight in the infield. Meanwhile, Richard Petty cruised by to his sixth Daytona win.

A big part of Richard's success resulted from his close family ties. Though Lee taught his son tough lessons, he always supported Richard. "I got more nervous when he was out there and I was in the pits than when I drove," Lee Petty said. Richard's wife, mother, and brother Maurice were also in on the family racing business. And now Richard's son Kyle continues the Petty tradition.

Many have called Richard the greatest stock car racer of all time. "I don't know about greatness," Richard has said. "That's for others to decide. My daddy was a race driver, so I became a race driver. If he'd been a grocer, I'd have been a grocer. I just go out and do the best I can and often as not it's been good enough. Oh, I have pride in my record, but I really just consider myself a workin' stiff."

A workin' stiff who will always be known as the king of stock car racing!

CHAPTER 10

CAR WARS

The big U.S. car companies have always had mixed feelings about racing. The engineers use motor sport to test out new ideas. It makes their jobs more fun.

Business types don't like the cost of racing. But they love the added sales that racing brings. "Win on Sunday, sell on Monday" is one of the oldest sayings in the car business. And business people worry that if other companies race and they don't, sales will be lost.

In 1957 the car company executives tried to put their worries to rest by making an agreement. Nobody would race. That way, nobody would get the extra sales. The agreement was called the **AMA (Automobile Manufacturers' Association) ban.**

For a few years the ban seemed to work. But then those mixed feelings about racing cropped up again. The new market of younger buyers was just too big a target. The carmakers watched each other like nervous gunfighters. Each waited for the others to make the first move back to racing. The scene was being set for an incredible horsepower shootout.

Pontiac fired first. For years General Motors' mid-size, mid-price division had been known as a maker of dull cars. But then a sharp new boss came in. He decided to change that image by creating a company that could advertise, "We build excitement!"

Suddenly Pontiacs began appearing on NASCAR tracks. They were driven by stars like Fireball Roberts. Then Chevrolets started racing, too.

The official story was that these cars were entered by private owners.

The massive V-8's in NASCAR racers start as stock blocks but are tuned by expert mechanics. A good crew can pop in a new engine in minutes.

The car companies had nothing to do with the cars. But somehow these private owners were able to get their hands on special speed parts made only by the factory. To prove this, Ford got hold of a Pontiac racing engine and looked inside. It was totally unlike the street motor, Ford said, and broke at least 14 NASCAR rules!

Soon after that, a Ford executive was sent down to watch the first Daytona 500. When he reached his seat, he found himself surrounded by top Chevy and Pontiac bosses. They even bought him lunch!

"I knew then the AMA ban was as good as dead," the man reported when he returned to Ford's headquarters. Someone at Ford then wrote to GM asking flat out if the company was back in racing. There was no answer. Ford decided that meant yes. The war was on!

As much as on the track, the war was fought in the engine lab. At first, each company just kept making its engines bigger. Massive, 390-**cubic-inch** motors grew to 406 inches. Then they got even bigger, becoming 427s and 440s. Only the basic engine designs stayed stock.

But in 1963 Chevy showed up at Daytona with a new kind of motor. All American V-8s of the time were **pushrod** engines. They had long rods that stuck straight up from the cylinders. The rods helped open and close the valves. And the rods were always neatly lined up in a row.

On the new Chevy engine, the pushrods stuck out at all kinds of crazy angles, like the quills on a porcupine. The engine became known as the **porcupine V-8 engine.**

Once trials started, Ford learned that the design was as fast as it was different. Chevies could run laps at 164 mph, compared with the best Ford speeds of 161. That may not sound like much difference. But in a one-hour race, a Chevy would finish 3 miles ahead of a Ford. Nobody at Ford wanted that finish on the evening news.

As it happened, the 1963 Chevies broke down. Ford won Daytona that year. But Ford knew that the GM motor was more powerful. Once its troubles were sorted out, it would be hard to beat.

Then there was Chrysler. Although the smallest of the Big Three automakers, the company had always had great engineering. Back in the 1950s, the company had built a powerful car called the Chrysler 300. This brutal machine regularly ate Fords and Chevies for lunch on the old beach and dirt tracks. The 300's winning edge was its incredibly strong engine.

This engine was known as the **hemi.** The name came from the design of its firing chambers, which were dome-shaped. The engineers call it hemispherical. The engine was costly to build and was no longer made. But Ford and GM knew that Chrysler hadn't forgotten how to make it!

Then, in 1964, Plymouths and Dodges suddenly began to go a lot faster than they ever had before. The other carmakers quickly found out why.

The hemi was back! It was bigger and badder than ever! It was as if some creature from a horror movie had returned. Other drivers began calling Chrysler's monster powerplant the King Kong engine.

Suddenly, speeds on the top NASCAR tracks topped 170 mph. Faced with such threats, Ford now reached into its bag of tricks. Out came another entirely new engine design. Ford had built the world's first **overhead cam** stock car racing V-8.

In an overhead cam engine, the parts that open and close the valves are placed directly over the valves. This allows the valves to work faster for more power. Overhead cam design gave the beefy new Ford V-8 more than 500 horsepower!

By this time, each factory was accusing the others of cheating. Each carmaker was demanding that everybody else be punished. Something had to be done, and Bill France had to do it. He banned the Ford overhead cam engine altogether and put serious limits on how Chrysler could use the hemi. (GM pulled the porcupine on its own.) Chrysler got mad and dropped out of NASCAR for a year. Later, Ford pulled out for a time. But it seemed that peace had been restored.

For a while.

Actually, peace lasted only until the factories figured they could get a leg up on each other with body design.

When the first speedways opened, drivers found that racing at over 150 mph was a lot like flying. The way the air flowed over a car could mean the difference between winning and losing. Boxy cars needed far more power than streamlined ones to gain speed. Simply lowering the body an inch or two could be a winning edge.

This Superbird is powered by the incredible hemi engine.

The factories began to put this knowledge to use. Suddenly, some of their new models had streamlined **fastback** roofs. These roofs formed smooth, downhill curves from windshields to the back bumpers. The factories spent a lot of money to create this style. But showroom shoppers preferred the boxy look.

It was legal to have a streamlined race model if the company sold a similar street model. But NASCAR inspectors thought that some of the racers

seemed just a little too slick. They got out special measuring devices called **templates**. Using templates, they checked the body shapes. Sure enough, some of the teams were making illegal changes.

Streamlining reached its height with the Dodge Charger Daytona and Plymouth Road Runner Superbird models of 1970. Those cars were really designed for the superspeedways. But a number of them were sold for street use. You can still see them today at 1960s **muscle car** shows. And once you've seen one, you definitely won't forget it.

To the standard body, Chrysler added a guided-missile-shaped nose that stuck out about an extra 2 feet. The nose made parking nearly impossible. The headlights were sunk into the nose. And there was no grille. Instead, the motor sucked in air from below the body.

On the trunk, designers added a wing that would do a Boeing 747 proud. The car had a set of fat tires. And a 426-inch hemi V-8 engine was stuffed under that long hood. These were the ultimate stock cars of their time!

What they really showed, though, was how far from stock these stock cars had come. Big-time stock car racing was now just another form of specialized motor sports. The cars may be called Thunderbird or Grand Prix, just like street machines. But under the nameplates, they're made for racing only. The great factory war of the 1960s made NASCAR racing what it is today.

CHAPTER 11

A MATTER OF ENGINE-ERING

The next morning you head over to your team's garage to see how things are going. One of the cars is getting an engine change. Watching the specialists, you realize that an engine is the only thing that's stock on a stock car: The engines still come from the factory whose name is on the car.

From the factory, engines go to an expert engine builder to be prepared for racing. But not every engine sent by the factory makes the race. Your builder picked through 15 blocks and kept the few that are especially well built.

Then the real work began. The builder checked and polished every major part, then installed special racing-quality pistons, shafts, balancers, filters, and other parts. The tiny stickers on your racer's fenders list all the companies that have parts in your engine. There are dozens of them!

The racers that run at Daytona are limited in engine size to 358 cubic inches. That's about the size of a Corvette street engine. In a Vette, an engine of that size might produce 250 horsepower. But thanks to your builder, your engine pumps close to 700 horses! After today's race, however, the engine will probably have to be totally rebuilt. The race will be that demanding.

Standing in the garage, you learn firsthand that there's nothing quite like the sound of a big-block NASCAR engine. At idle, its rumpa-rumpa rhythm promises the ride of your life. But it's a different matter when you touch the throttle. Then the beast winds up to a 6,000-rpm scream that shakes the whole building. The sound is often compared to thunder, and that's true from the grandstands. But from where you're standing, the sound is more like an endless bomb explosion—which is why you're wearing foam earplugs.

THE "TIDE" OF VICTORY

Bill France retired as head of NASCAR in 1970. His son, Bill France Jr. took his place. The change was like one door opening while another closed. Bill Sr. had come from a world of ex-bootleggers, dirt and sand races, and rules made to be broken. From that wild mixture he'd created modern stock car racing. It was something auto lovers nationwide could be proud of.

Now Bill Jr. had to make stock car racing grow from there.

He and other NASCAR officials knew they would not have much help from the car companies. In the 1970s, two things happened that almost drove the automakers out of racing.

One was that the government finally began to enact new safety laws. Lawmakers weren't bothered by racing but by something else. Some 50,000 Americans were dying in traffic accidents each year. Legislators put laws on the books that forced auto companies to build safer cars.

The other thing that happened was a war between Israel and the Arab states of the Middle East. The Arabs believed that the United States was Israel's ally. So they cut off part of America's oil supply. With gasoline hard to find, buyers suddenly wanted cars that got good gas mileage. (NASCAR even shortened the 1974 Daytona 500 to 450 miles to show it cared about the problem!)

Because of these two developments, Detroit's engineers had to make massive changes in their regular models. There was no time or money left for racing. If NASCAR was to survive, a new source of big-company help had to be found.

Stock car racing did have one thing on its side: The superspeedways and factory battles had attracted millions of new fans. A few hundred might have watched a race in the early 1950s. Now 100,000 or more often packed into the great speedway events.

Major races, like the Daytona 500, were also broadcast on television. Those big-fendered racing cars were on TV for hours at a time. Millions of viewers watched the cars zoom around the track. And those viewers bought lots of products besides cars. That made advertisers sit up and take notice.

Eventually, someone in the ad business had an idea: Use the broad sides and hood of a NASCAR stock car as a rolling billboard. Their products would have a free ad every time the car passed a TV camera.

This wasn't a new idea to garages and auto-parts makers. They'd advertised on stock cars for years. But now the makers of other kinds of products jumped in. And every one of them was a business giant. Suddenly there was a Tide laundry detergent racing team, a Mello Yello soft-drink special, and a Kodak-film car. There were so many racers carrying the names of beer companies that you could get woozy counting them!

Some of the biggest advertising deals were made with the tobacco companies. NASCAR's top string of races (which includes the Daytona 500) became the Winston Cup series. It was named after a brand of cigarette.

Some critics have always felt that racing should not be connected with cigarettes and alcohol (even though stock car racing started from bootlegging). But others point out that these products are legal. And the money

Richard Petty shows off his racer...and the names of his sponsors.

paid by sponsors goes for improvements that are needed to keep the sport growing.

There have been many improvements in stock car racing. New super-speedways at Atlanta, Georgia, and Talladega, Alabama, have joined Daytona in hosting 200-mph events. Some 30 races are scheduled in the top **late-model series** each year. And dozens of lesser events for older-model stock and modified cars are also held.

Over the years, NASCAR has grown to be more than a southern series. Races are now held as far north as Pennsylvania, Delaware, and New Hampshire. And in 1994, NASCAR stock cars started racing at the most famous track in America—the Indianapolis Motor Speedway, home of the Indy 500!

PIT ACTION

At Daytona there's as much action in the pits as there is on the track. And you know that what happens there is vitally important. Your pit crew can change 4 tires and gas the car up in 15-20 seconds.

Tires have to be changed often. Your team has about 20 tires on hand for today's race. The cars only make left turns on the big speedways. This puts the weight and pressure on the outside, or right, tires. So right-side tires are changed more often than left-side tires.

Changing tires is hard, hot work! The wheel-tire units weigh 90 pounds each. And a tire can heat up to 200 degrees. Just from riding in the steamy cockpit, you can understand how!

Gas is dumped in from 11-gallon, 80-pound cans. Your crew members hold the cans over their heads as the fuel drains into the car. The rules allow five people in the pit to work on the car. If you want your windshield cleaned, it's done by someone holding a long pole over the pit wall.

Your crew has brought most of what it needs with it. A tire company provides the wheels right at the raceway. But spare engines and other key parts travel with you and the rest of the team in giant trucks. The trucks are air-conditioned garages on wheels, complete with machine tools and

The real key to winning can be a fast, talented pit crew.

engine lifts. Some even have comfortable lounges stocked with food and cool drinks. But not yours. You're racing with a small team that can't afford such luxury.

Racing at Daytona costs a lot. Your sponsor has spent about $100,000 on your car. And that doesn't include what they pay you and your crew.

Whatever it costs, a top team is worth it. A good car and good pit work can make a championship. Bad work can break one.

How good is your team? You're about to find out.

FUTURE STOCK!

You can imagine racing at Daytona any time you like. But you won't be able to race there at least until you reach legal driving age. What will Daytona and the NASCAR world be like in the twenty-first century? Most likely, the race cars will improve along with cars in general. But they'll never be as high-tech as Indy or Grand Prix machines. NASCAR people tend to make changes slowly.

NASCAR teams also tend to be happy with their big ol' rear-wheel-drive V-8s. They know this layout like a favorite easy chair. Chances are that the same basic layout will be racing in the year 2000.

There will be improvements. Cars may feature more electronics in the engine and better metals in the chassis. And tires get better all the time.

With the high speeds that Daytona is famous for, safety is a number one concern. Engineers are working to make stock cars as safe as possible, complete with fuel cells, roll cages, and tough Lexan windshields.

Aside from supporting car improvements, both NASCAR and its teams are paying more attention to the environment. The stock car racing world recently hooked up with a large company that specializes in recycling used cleaning liquids and oil. So these things will no longer be thrown away.

There will also be improvements for the fans. Even now, drivers are hired by the TV networks to wear tiny helmet TV cameras. These allow viewers to see the action the way the drivers do. Such equipment will get smaller and lighter. And when three-dimensional TV becomes real, viewers will get the feel of the action, too.

The races will also be easier to find on TV. The Nashville Network (TNN) and ESPN carry some of the races now, and the big networks sign on for superspeedway events like Daytona. But new cable systems will carry up to 500 channels. There could even be a NASCAR channel, with stock car racing 24 hours a day!

The races will be easier to get to in person, as well. Stock car racing will always be as much a part of the South as grits and gravy. But as more people look in on TV, interest is growing in the rest of the nation. A superspeedway might even be built in your hometown!

CHAPTER 15

RACE DAY!

Up north, the February snows are falling. But here in Daytona, more than 150,000 fans settle in under warm, sunny skies. Things are going to get a lot hotter soon—and we're not talking about the weather.

Down on the track, you belt into your car and wait quietly while bands play and officials make speeches. You know the ability of the cars and dri-

NASCAR thunder roars again!

vers around you. You know the history of this place. And you wonder if you're good enough to be part of it.

Then comes the signal to start the engines. And the sound of rolling thunder is again heard at the beach. You fall in behind the pace car and begin to roll toward the green flag. In the 500 wild miles to come, anything can happen.

Are you really "out to win"?

GLOSSARY

AMA (Automobile Manufacturers' Association) ban A 1957 agreement among the American carmakers not to race.

banked Sloped, describes a roadway in a curve.

bootlegging Manufacturing, selling, or transporting illegal liquor.

chassis The frame and major mechanical parts of a car, including the engine, transmission, and suspension.

cubic inch A measure of an engine's size.

draft The wind effect created by one race car at high speeds. The car behind it can take advantage of the "hole" that the other car has punched in the air.

fastback An auto body style in which the roof slopes down from the windshield to the rear bumper.

fuel cell A rubberized foam-filled bag that holds fuel. It helps to prevent fire in a crash.

hemi A powerful Chrysler engine, named after its dome-shaped (hemispherical) firing chambers.

late-model series A series of races held for recent model automobiles.

Lexan A tough, clear plastic sheet used in place of glass on race car windows.

locknut To fasten with a nut that's constructed so that it locks in place when screwed against another part in an engine.

muscle car A 2-door American car sports coupe with a powerful engine. Muscle cars are built for performance.

NASCAR (National Association for Stock Car Auto Racing) The group that controls most major stock car racing in the United States.

overhead cam A system that opens and closes engine fuel valves faster than pushrod designs. The design allows for higher engine speed and more power.

porcupine V-8 engine A 1960s Chevrolet experimental motor. The name referred to the way the pushrods stuck out of the engine at unusual angles.

pushrod An engine part that opens and closes the valves.

roll cage A framework of metal tubes over and around a driver in a racing car. It is designed to protect the driver in a crash or a rollover.

superspeedway Very large, high-speed racetrack, often with banked turns.

template An instrument used to measure car parts.

trioval A triangle-shaped racecourse, such as the Daytona Speedway.

Winston Cup NASCAR's top stock car racing series.

INDEX

AMA ban 28
Atlanta 40

banked 4
bootlegging 12, 13, 14, 36

Campbell, Sir Malcolm 8, 9, 10, 12

Daytona Beach 6, 7, 12, 14
drafting 5

fastback 31
France, Bill, Jr. 36
France, Bill, Sr. 10, 11, 14, 20, 21, 22, 36
fuel cell 24, 43

Guthrie, Janet 16

hemi 31, 32, 34

Lexan 4, 43
Lockhart, Frank 8, 12

NASCAR 6, 10, 11, 20, 21, 22, 26, 30, 31, 32, 34, 36, 37, 40, 43, 44

Olds, Ransom E. 7
Ormand Beach 6, 7
overhead cam 31

Petty, Kyle 27
Petty, Lee 22, 25, 27
Petty, Richard 23, 25, 26, 27, 28
porcupine engine 30
pushrod 30

Roberts, Glenn "Fireball" 22, 28
roll cage 24, 43

Seagrave, Henry O. 8, 9, 12
superspeedway 20, 22, 33, 37

Talledaga 40
trioval 21
Turner, Curtis "Pops" 18, 19

Winton, Alexander 7
Winston Cup 6, 37

Yarborough, Cale 26